Why Not?

Why Not?

Sylvia A. Hofsepian

Illustrated by Friso Henstra

Four Winds Press   New York
Collier Macmillan Canada   Toronto
Maxwell Macmillan International Publishing Group
New York   Oxford   Singapore   Sydney

Four Winds Press
Macmillan Publishing Company
866 Third Avenue, New York, NY 10022
Collier Macmillan Canada, Inc.
1200 Eglinton Avenue East
Suite 200
Don Mills, Ontario M3C 3N1
Printed and bound in Singapore
First American Edition
10 9 8 7 6 5 4 3 2 1
The text of this book is set in 15 point Fournier.
The illustrations are rendered in pen and ink and watercolor.

Library of Congress Cataloging-in-Publication Data
Hofsepian, Sylvia A. Why not? / Sylvia A. Hofsepian :
illustrated by Friso Henstra.—
1st American ed.   p.   cm.
Summary: A solemn man who is lonely gets
a cat for company, but one thing leads to
another and soon he gets a wife as well.
ISBN 0-02-743980-1
[1. Cats—Fiction.   2. Loneliness—Fiction.]
I. Henstra, Friso, ill.   II. Title.
PZ7.H6798Wh   1991   [E]—dc20
89-39333

With thanks to Cindy
—S.H.
For Tessa, Maaike,
Sylvia, and Chris
—F.H.

Once there was a solemn man whose wife had died and whose children had all grown up and left home. At times he was lonely, so he decided to get a little cat to keep him company.

"Why not?" he said to himself. "It will harm no one and might be rather cozy."

He looked here and there in the village but couldn't find just the cat he was looking for. "When the bread woman comes in her housecart, I'll ask her if she knows of a cat," he told himself. "She chats with everyone and knows all the goings-on."

The solemn man waited for the housecart with flowers in the window boxes. When it stopped at his gate, he bought his bread and invited the cheerful bread woman in for tea.

He put the tea kettle on, and the cheerful woman

cut thick slices of fresh warm bread to eat with sweet butter and tart marmalade. Then, over tea, the cheerful woman told all the news of the village.

"Farmer Burns tripped over a pig and hurt his leg," she said.

"Hmmmm," said the solemn man.

"The Smith twins have the measles," she said.

"Hmmmm," said he, half listening.

The cheerful woman went on and on. When she stopped, the solemn man told how he had looked for a cat but had been unable to find one that suited him.

"Take my cat," cried the cheerful woman. "I have two cats, and one of them is too noisy for me and my little housecart. She needs to run about and poke her nose into this and that. Please take her."

"Why not?" said the solemn man. "Perhaps my house is too quiet. She will be good company for me. Let me see her."

The little cat was just the cat the solemn man had been looking for. She was small and dainty and tawny colored, with eyes as blue as a bright winter sky. When the solemn man picked her up, she jumped on his shoulder and rubbed her face against his ear.

After thanking the cheerful woman, the solemn man carried the little cat into his cottage and set her down on a red velvet cushion. "What shall I call you, my little one?" he asked. And since he had been reading a French story the night before, he named her Ma Petite, which means "my little one."

The solemn man lit a fire in the fireplace, poured cream into a blue and white bowl, and set about making some stew for his supper. "How do you like your new home, Ma Petite?" he asked.

"Mowww," said Ma Petite in a loud voice. She jumped off the cushion and ran around the cottage, poking her nose into this and that and meowing all the while. Before long she had been in every corner of the cottage and knew what and where everything was.

"Well, why not?" the solemn man said. "It is grand to be quiet, but a little noise once in a while harms no one."

He set the bowl of cream on the floor and sat down to supper.

"Mowww," Ma Petite said loudly, and sprang lightly up on the table.

"Sooo," he said, "you want some of my supper. Why not?" He put some stew in a dish on the floor, and Ma Petite jumped down from the table and ate every bit.

After supper the solemn man sat before the fire and read his book while Ma Petite curled up on his lap and went to sleep.

When it was time for bed, he gently lifted the sleeping cat and laid her on the red velvet cushion. But as soon as he turned around, Ma Petite followed him into the bedroom. She jumped on the bed, curled up in the blankets at the solemn man's feet, and purred until she fell asleep.

The solemn man nodded. "Why not?" he said to himself. "It isn't what I had planned, but it harms no one and it certainly is cozy." And he went to sleep and slept better than he had in a long time.

Days went by. The little cat stayed with the solemn man always and talked to him in her high shrill voice. She told him when to get up and when to go to bed. She ate what he ate and slept on his bed every night. The solemn man was never lonely.

Then came the day that he set aside to pick up supplies in the village. He would be gone from early morning until well into the evening. "You stay here, Ma Petite. I shall be back before you know it," he said as he locked the door.

But Ma Petite didn't want to be alone. She flew from window to window and screamed and screeched. She clawed at the door and climbed up the curtains.

When the solemn man got home he was startled to see the cottage in shambles: the furniture was upset, the curtains were torn, and the doors and windows were frightfully scratched.

He became more troubled when he saw Ma Petite. She limped to the door when he entered and dropped like a rag doll at his feet. For two days she slept, never eating or making a sound; her throat was too sore from all that screeching.

"How is the cat?" asked the cheerful bread woman on her next visit.

Fine," said the solemn man, for Ma Petite was herself again.

But when he went to the village once more, the same thing happened—only worse. This time the little cat slept for three days afterward.

"I cannot let this go on any longer!" he said to himself. "I brought this little cat home so *I* would not be lonely. Now *she* is sick from loneliness. Whatever shall I do?"

When the cheerful woman came in her housecart, he again asked her in for tea and fresh-baked bread.

"Farmer Anderson was up all night with his sick horse," the cheerful woman began.

"Hmmmm," said the solemn man.

"They say we are in for a bad winter," she said.

"But what shall I do about my poor cat?" he cried, unable to listen any longer. He told her all about Ma Petite.

"Take my second cat," said the cheerful woman after thinking a bit. "My housecart is drafty now, and the nights are getting cold. I will miss her, but she will be warm and cozy in your cottage."

So the solemn man thanked the cheerful woman and carried the second cat to the snug little cottage. Because he had been reading a Russian book the night before, he named her Tashkin, which means "little Tasha."

She was small and dainty and blue-eyed like the first cat, but while Ma Petite was bossy, this cat was shy; while Ma Petite was noisy, Tashkin was quiet. She was not interested in knowing what and where everything was, but preferred instead to sleep on the red velvet cushion in a patch of sunshine or to chase her tiny fur ball under a chair or to drink cream from the blue and white bowl.

"Why not?" said the solemn man, looking a bit less solemn. "This is not what I expected, but it harms no one and it is rather cozy."

On the bread woman's next visit, she asked, "How are the two cats?"

"Fine," he said.

"I am glad," she said, "for I have decided to go and live with my daughter for the winter, and she does not like my little cats."

The cheerful woman did not look so cheerful. "This is the last time I shall sell you bread until spring comes, my friend."

"There, there," said the solemn man. He could see she was not happy about going, and he was sorry that he could not help her as she had helped him.

After supper, he settled down to read in his rocking chair by the fire with Ma Petite on his lap. Tashkin napped on her red velvet cushion on the hearth. Presently Tashkin was awakened by the howling of the wind and the pounding of rain against the cottage. Without making a sound, she left the red cushion and climbed up into the solemn man's lap beside Ma Petite. There was plenty of room.

Nonetheless, Ma Petite sprang up, spitting and hissing. She flew at little Tashkin and slapped her again and again. The solemn man was quite startled, and Tashkin was so frightened that she hid under a chair until long after Ma Petite had gone back to sleep.

Every evening after that, while the nights grew colder and the wind whistled in the chimney, Tashkin crept sadly to the red velvet cushion. Not again did she dare set foot in the solemn man's lap.

"Oh, my," he said. "I brought Ma Petite home so I wouldn't be lonely. I brought Tashkin home so Ma Petite wouldn't be lonely. Now Tashkin is lonely. What shall I do?"

He thought of the cheerful woman. "She helped me before. She would know what to do," he said to himself. "I wish she were here. Why didn't I ask her not to go? Now I must wait until spring to see her again."

Clapping his book shut, he started up from his chair, sending Ma Petite leaping to the fireplace mantel and Tashkin dashing under a chair. Back and forth he paced, muttering, "Why did I let her go? Why? Why? Why?"

Suddenly an idea popped into his head. A hint of a smile appeared at the corners of his mouth, and a twinkle brightened his eyes. "Why must I wait until spring? I will go and see her myself. Why not?"

The very next morning he went to see the cheerful woman.

"Please," he said gently. "Don't stay away. Come and be my wife."

The cheerful woman thought a bit and looked cheerful again. "Why not?" she said slowly. "Why not?"

The solemn man built a barn for the horse and the housecart. The cheerful woman made new white curtains for the cottage. On some days they hitched the horse to the housecart and drove to the village to hear the goings-on.

And every evening during that long, cold winter, when the wind beat against the house, the solemn man and his wife sat in their rocking chairs before a roaring fire. Ma Petite curled up contentedly in the solemn man's lap and Tashkin snuggled in the cheerful woman's lap.

"Goodness me!" the solemn man would often chuckle. "I expected to spend the rest of my days alone. But now I have a whole new family."

"Why not?" his cheerful wife would reply. "It harms no one, and it certainly *is* cozy."